I0589005

If God Wanted Us To Fly, He Would Have Given Us Wings!

by Kitty Burns

‖SAMUEL FRENCH‖

ISBN 978-0-573-70134-4

www.concordtheatricals.com
www.concordtheatricals.co.uk

FOR PRODUCTION INQUIRIES

UNITED STATES AND CANADA
info@concordtheatricals.com
1-866-979-0447

UNITED KINGDOM AND EUROPE
licensing@concordtheatricals.co.uk
020-7054-7298

Each title is subject to availability from Concord Theatricals Corp.,
depending upon country of performance. Please be aware that *IF GOD
WANTED US TO FLY, HE WOULD HAVE GIVEN US WINGS!* may not
be licensed by Concord Theatricals Corp. in your territory. Professional
and amateur producers should contact the nearest Concord Theatricals
Corp. office or licensing partner to verify availability.

Three One Act Plays:

THIS PLAY IS DEDICATED TO

JENNIFER ROPERS

TERMINAL TERROR

CHARACTERS

AGENT / PILOT:
  About 30 Years Old – Anal Retentive
JENNIFER SUMNER:
  Early 20's – "Princess" Attitude
LIZ DAVIDSON:
  About 50 Years Old – Bossy, Overbearing
JACK DAVIDSON:
  About 50 Years Old – Uncouth, Earthy
HERMAN SCHNEIDER:
  30-50 Years Old – Polyester, Pushy Salesman

ORIGINAL CAST OF TERMINAL TERROR
Produced by The Rasputin Theatre Company
At The Studio Eremos in San Francisco, CA
June 8-16, 1991

CAST MEMBERS

Pilot/Agent . . . . Brendon Nash
Jennifer Sumner . . . . Liz Carr
Liz Davidson . . . . Donna Canali
Jack Davidson . . . . David Picariello
Herman Schneider . . . . Leon Brenton
Girl with Barf Bag . . . . Kitty Burns
Director . . . . Jean Stein
Sound Production . . . . Brendon Nash
Lighting . . . . Leonid Turkin
Lighting Assistant . . . . Lisa Woodward

Scene One

(JENNIFER SUMNER enters the lounge area of JFK International Airport in New York, Phoenix Airlines area, where there is one check-in desk with an Agent behind it and walks over to him. The Agent is changing the flight number and time on the boarding sign behind the desk and is wearing a black suit and white carnation.)

JENNIFER: Excuse me. *(The AGENT turns around)* Hi. I have a reservation on Flight 352 going to New London, Connecticut.

AGENT: Name?

JENNIFER: Jennifer Sumner.

AGENT: Ticket, please. *(JENNIFER hands him her ticket)* Smoking or non-smoking?

JENNIFER: Non-smoking.

AGENT: That was a joke. The plane only seats eight people. The whole thing is a non-smoking section.

JENNIFER: Oh. That's OK. I don't smoke anyway. *(As she is talking, JACK and LIZ enter the lounge area. LIZ sits down and JACK stands behind JENNIFER. JENNIFER pauses for a few seconds, thinking about what the AGENT just said)* Did you say the plane only seats eight people?

AGENT: Yes. I guess you've never flown with us before.

JENNIFER: No. Actually, I've never flown with anybody before.

AGENT: This is your first flight?

JENNIFER: Yep.
AGENT: Laughs to himself.

(The kind of laugh that makes JENNIFER nervous.)

JENNIFER: It's so empty in here. Am I too early?
AGENT: No. You're right on time. So, you've never flown before?

(Reaches over the desk and picks a piece of lint off her coat.)

JENNIFER: No. I've never had a reason or frankly the desire to fly.
AGENT: What brings you here today?
JENNIFER: I have to go to Connecticut for my sister's wedding.
AGENT: That's a nice reason for a first flight.
JENNIFER: To tell you the truth, I'm not real crazy about doing this. I don't like the idea of being 30,000 feet off the ground in a machine!
AGENT: Now, don't be nervous. You have absolutely nothing to worry about. Phoenix Airlines has been in business for over 50 years. Our planes may be small, but they're quite durable, and our pilots are among the best in the business. Now, you just have a seat over there, and our ground hostess will let you know when it is time to board. *(Hands her the ticket)* Oh, I should warn you. There is no bathroom on board, so if you need to go, better do it now.
JENNIFER: Thank you.

(Goes and sits down in the seat across from the woman.)

AGENT: Thank you.

(Takes a cloth out of the desk and wipes off the counter. JACK moves up to the counter and he hands the AGENT his ticket and they talk quietly.)

LIZ: Hello.

JENNIFER: Hi.

LIZ: Do you fly very often?

JENNIFER: *(Nervously)* No. Do you?

LIZ: Oh yes. I love it. My husband and I live in Connecticut and come to New York all the time. We're retired now, and come to see all the new Broadway shows. On this trip, we saw the David Letterman show. We're both big fans of his. Wait till you retire. I bet you'll travel a lot too.

JENNIFER: Oh no, not me. This is my first flight and it's going to be my last. I've always been afraid to fly.

LIZ: Oh, that's too bad. Are you afraid now?

JENNIFER: Petrified!

LIZ: Believe me, you have nothing to worry about. We fly all the time. This is only the second time we've taken Phoenix Airlines, but the last time we had great service and a very comfortable ride. You couldn't be in better hands.

JENNIFER: *(Looks puzzled)* How strange. For a minute there, what you just said sounded vaguely familiar.

(JACK comes over and sits by LIZ. AGENT wipes off counter when he leaves.)

LIZ: All set?

JACK: *(Not happy)* Yeah.

LIZ: Good. Honey. this young lady is flying for the first time today.

JACK: Oh really?

(Not interested.)
(Picks up newspaper and starts reading it.)

LIZ: How long are you going to be in Connecticut?

JENNIFER: Just for the weekend. I'm going to be in my sister's wedding.

LIZ: That's wonderful!

AGENT: Good evening ladies and gentlemen. Flight 352 non-stop service from New London has been delayed due to adverse weather conditions. The plane will be arriving in approximately 15 minutes and you will be boarding shortly thereafter.

(HERMAN enters, wearing a plaid suit and carrying two small suitcases. He runs up to AGENT's desk.)

HERMAN: Thank God the flight's delayed. I was afraid I was going to miss it.

(Hands AGENT his ticket.)

AGENT: No, you've even got a little time to relax before departure.

(They talk quietly while AGENT works on HERMAN's ticket.)

JENNIFER: *(Looking out window)* I sure wish it would stop raining. How is that little plane going to stay up in a storm like this?

LIZ: Don't worry. If it was raining too hard or was too windy, they wouldn't fly. The pilot wants to land safely just as much as the passengers do.

JENNIFER: I guess so.

LIZ: What part of New York are you from?

JENNIFER: For the last 10 years I've lived on Long Island, but right now I'm going to NYU.

LIZ: Cause you look awfully familiar to me.

JENNIFER: No, I don't think we've ever met.

LIZ: Oh well. By the way, my name is Liz Davidson, and this is my husband, Jack.

JENNIFER: Nice to meet you. I'm Jennifer Sumner.

ALL: Hi.

LIZ: You know, I've been flying all my life.

JACK: *(Not looking up from his paper, interrupts her)* Yeah, but she's only been up in a plane twice.

(Laughs to himself.)

LIZ: *(Gives JACK a dirty look and repeats irritated)* I've been flying all my life and love it. It's the most relaxing and fun form of travel there is.

JACK: Yeah, where'd you read that?

LIZ: It's true. Once you're on board, you can put your seat back and go to sleep if you want to. You can read. On the longer flights, you can even listen to music or watch a movie. *(To JACK irritated)* You can't do that on a train.

JACK: *(To JENNIFER)* I wanted to take the train.

LIZ: You always want to take the train.

JACK: That's right. Trains don't take you up 50,000 feet in the air!

LIZ: Planes don't go any higher than 36,000 feet.

JACK: Whatever! Either way, it's a long way up and a long way down!

LIZ: Would you stop that! You're scaring her.

JACK: Hell, even John Madden won't get in an airplane. He bought his own bus so he wouldn't have to fly.

LIZ: Well, John Madden's a wimp!

(Everyone, including the AGENT and HERMAN, looks up and stares at LIZ as if they are shocked by what she just said.)

JACK: You don't see life insurance booths in train stations and bus terminals, do you?

HERMAN: *(Turns around at AGENT's desk)* Did someone say, "Life insurance?" *(Walks quickly over to people and takes business cards out of his inner pocket and hands one to each person)* Allow me to introduce myself. My name is Herman Schneider.

(AGENT wipes off counter when HERMAN leaves and continues cleaning around counter.)

JACK: *(Looks at the card and hands it back to HERMAN)* We have Prudential.

HERMAN: *(Walks over to JENNIFER)* Well, little lady, what about you?

JENNIFER: What about me?

HERMAN: Do you have life insurance?

JENNIFER: No. I'm college student. What do I need with life insurance?

HERMAN: Sweetie, everybody needs life insurance. You have bills, don't you?

JENNIFER: Just tuition and one credit card.

HERMAN: Well, Babe, do you want your parents to get stuck paying off your debts?

JENNIFER: I'm going to be paying off my debts. I'm 24 years old and in perfect health. I plan to be around for a long time.

HERMAN: Honey, Baby, we all plan to be around for a long time, but that's why I'm in business. You know what they say about the best laid plans. One little 747 goes down, and all of a sudden, 250 people who planned to be around for a long time bite the big one!

LIZ: Would you shut up! She's scared enough as it is. Jennifer, don't you pay any attention to him. We're going to be just fine.

AGENT: *(To HERMAN)* Sir, you forgot your ticket.

HERMAN: Oh, yeah, won't get far without that.

(Goes up to AGENT and gets ticket.)

AGENT: And you forgot to check your bags at the ticket counter.

HERMAN: I'm not checking these. This is my carry-on luggage.

AGENT: Carry-on luggage?

HERMAN: That's right.

AGENT: And just where do you plan to carry these on?

HERMAN: On the plane – where do you think?

AGENT: Sir, have you ever flown on our airline before?

HERMAN: No.

AGENT: I didn't think so. This plane has eight seats in it, ten if you count the pilot and co-pilot. There are no overhead compartments, and there is no room for anything, including your feet, under the seats. There is nowhere to put carry-on luggage.

HERMAN: That's crazy! What kind of a plane can't accommodate carry-on luggage?

AGENT: A small plane. Carry-on luggage is meant for airliners. This is a puddle jumper.

HERMAN: A what?

AGENT: Never mind. Now, let's just get a few things straightened out here and you can bring your bags to the ticket counter.

HERMAN: What do you mean, "Get a few things straightened out?"

AGENT: For starters, this ticket is a mess. I'm going to void it out and issue a new one.

HERMAN: That's not necessary.

AGENT: Yes it is. You can hardly read it because the ink is smudged, the copy is torn, and the date is wrong, and I refuse to scratch out or write over anything.

HERMAN: God, do you have to be such a damned perfectionist?

AGENT: Yes, I do. *(Hands him a new ticket)* There, now hurry up and get your luggage to the ticket counter so they can load it with everyone else's.*(HERMAN walks out and AGENT wipes off the counter, then says over the loud speaker)* Good evening, ladies and gentlemen. Flight 352, non-stop service from New London has been delayed due to adverse weather conditions. The Plane will arriving in approximately 15 minutes and you will be boarding shortly thereafter.

JACK: That's what you said a few minutes ago.

AGENT: Well, I'm saying it again.

JENNIFER: *(To AGENT)* What's happening? Is something wrong with the plane?

AGENT: No, there's nothing wrong with the plane – just a little set back due to the storm – nothing to worry about.

JACK: *(To LIZ)* I told you we should have taken the train!

LIZ: Oh, be quiet! Between you and the Grim Reaper insurance salesman, you've got this poor girl scared to death!

JENNIFER: *(To LIZ)* You know, I really am getting scared. I don't think this was such a good idea. *(To JACK)* Is there a train going to Connecticut tonight?

JACK: I'm sure there is. If you find out, let me know. I'll go with you.

LIZ: *(Kicks JACK)* Knock it off! Relax – both of you! *(To JENNIFER)* Tell me about your sister's wedding. Are you going to be a bridesmaid?

JENNIFER: I'm going to be the Maid of Honor.

LIZ: Oh, that sounds lovely. I bet you're going to look beautiful. Have you ever been in a wedding before?

(HERMAN returns without his luggage.)

JENNIFER: No, this is my first. I'm having a lot of "firsts" this weekend.

LIZ: Yes, and you'll enjoy every one of them. When Jack and I got married, we had ...

AGENT: Ladies and gentlemen, Flight 352, non-stop service from New London, has just landed and is approaching the gate at this time. The passengers will be deplaning momentarily. We will prepare the plane for boarding as soon as possible. We regret the delay and thank you for your patience.

JENNIFER: I wish they'd hurry up. I'm dreading this enough as it is.

LIZ: Now, I told you, honey, you have nothing to worry about. We're going to have a wonderful flight. Besides, think of how awful it would be if we had to go everywhere by car or train or boat. Everything would be over crowded, and it would take forever. If you had to drive to Connecticut instead of fly, it would take you three hours. This way, you'll be there in a half hour, 45 minutes tops. Besides, I'm sure you've heard that it's safer to fly in a plane than it is to drive in a car.

JENNIFER: Yeah, I've heard that before.

LIZ: Well, it's true. Last year, there were thousands of car accidents in this country and only 7 airplane accidents. If I had my way ...

(At this point, the door from the outside opens, and five people enter, wet and mad. Four of them are making comments like, "I'll never fly again. I'm going to church tomorrow and thank God we landed safely. I can't believe we made it here in one piece. I'm surprised she's the only one who threw up. [pointing to the fifth girl] I thought for sure I was going to." Fifth girl slowly walks over to the Agent and hands him a used barf bag.)

GIRL: Hi. What do we do with these when we're done with them?

AGENT: Oh, I see you just flew on our airline. Give it to me and I'll put it in the back with the others.

(The GIRL hands him the barf bag and walks out.)

JENNIFER: OK, I've seen enough, I'm going home. I'll mail my sister her wedding present and tell her I'm deathly sick and can't make it.

LIZ: Now, lying to your sister isn't going to do anybody any good.

JENNIFER: If I get on that plane, I won't be lying!

(The PILOT enters from the outside. He goes up to the AGENT and as they're talking, they exchange coats. The

AGENT puts on the PILOT's cap. The PILOT goes behind the AGENT's desk.)

PILOT: *(EX-AGENT)* OK you guys, let's go.

JENNIFER: Wait a minute. What's going on here? Who are you?

PILOT: I'm your pilot, your co-pilot, your stewardess, your ground hostess. You name it, I'm it.

JENNIFER: I knew it. We're all going to die!

Scene Two

(Everyone is on board. HERMAN and LIZ are sitting by the windows.)

PILOT: Good evening, ladies and gentlemen, and welcome to Flight 352, non-stop service to New London, Connecticut. We will be climbing to an altitude of 20,000 feet, and our flying time is estimated at 35 minutes, so we should be arriving in New London at approximately 8:45 this evening. Please fasten your seat belts, and as we taxi down the runway, please familiarize yourselves with the safety instructions located in the seat pocket in front of you. In case of an emergency landing, you will be instructed according to the type of landing we are forced to make. Should we loose altitude at any time, oxygen masks will drop from overhead. Since we have a limited supply of masks, if there are more than four passengers on board, you will have to share. I hope you have a pleasant flight, and thank you for flying Phoenix Airlines.

ALL: What does he mean we'll have to share? We don't have enough masks?

JACK: Did you say we'll have to share oxygen masks?

PILOT: Well, let's see. *(Peeks at an index card in his coat pocket and repeats as if reading)* "Since we have a limited supply of masks, if there are more than four passengers on board, you will have to share. I hope you have a pleasant flight, and thank you" Yep, that's what I said.

JACK: How do you share an oxygen mask?

PILOT: I don't know. I've never had to do it before. I have my own. I guess it would be like sharing anything else. You take turns. In this case, you'd take turns breathing – one for you, one for me. *(Demonstrates with his mask)* But don't worry. There are only four of you on board, and besides, we hardly ever have to use these anyway.

(Puts his back where he got it.)

HERMAN: Hardly ever?

JACK: I'll get you for this, Liz.

PILOT: Prepare for take off. Everybody buckled up? Here we go. I love this part.

JACK: Someday, somehow, I'll get you for this.

LIZ: Now honey, just relax. Think about all the fun we had this weekend. Maybe try to take a little nap.

JACK: You know I can't sleep on these things.

LIZ: I know. Oh well, it'll all be over before you know it.

JACK: I guess so.

LIZ: *(Looks out window)* Hey, you know, this is weird.

JACK: What's that?

LIZ: Didn't he say we'd be flying at 20,000 feet?

JACK: Yeah.

LIZ: Well, it's still light out, but I don't see anything. I mean, at 20,000 feet, we should at least be able to see the clouds below us, and there should be plenty of them in this weather. And wouldn't you expect a lot of turbulence in a storm?

JACK: Hey, don't complain! Who wants turbulence?

LIZ: I'm not complaining. I don't want it. I just think it's odd that we're not having it. It's such a perfectly smooth ride.

JACK: Well, that's fine by me.

LIZ: I mean, look out the window. There's nothing.

JACK: That's OK. I'll take your word for it.

PILOT: *(Gets up and walks back to the passengers)* So, how we all doing? Everybody comfortable?

JENNIFER: What are you doing back here?

JACK: Yeah, get back up there and watch where we're going.

PILOT: Don't worry. We're on cruise control.

LIZ: You mean automatic pilot?

PILOT: Something like that.

JACK: Well, I don't like it. What if we hit something?

PILOT: Like what? A sparrow? I promise you – we're not going to hit anything and nothing is going to hit us. We've got the sky to ourselves.

JACK: Well, I'd feel a whole lot better if you were sitting up there at the controls.

PILOT: All right, if it'll make you happy.

(Goes back to cockpit.)

LIZ: You know he wouldn't have come back here if he didn't have everything under control.

JACK: Maybe if he had a co-pilot with him, I wouldn't mind, but not when he's up there alone.

LIZ: Remember the movie, "God Is My Co-Pilot"?

JACK: Oh, please! When I'm 20,000 feet in the air, I want to be able to see the guy behind the wheel.

PILOT: Well boys and girls, I have some good news and some bad news. The good news is we made it to New London. The bad news is we can't land in New London.

JACK: Why not?

PILOT: We have to circle.

JACK: What do you mean, circle?

PILOT: You know.

(Motions with his hands.)

JENNIFER: How long do we have to do that?

PILOT: I wish I knew.

JENNIFER: I swear to God, this is the worse night of my life. If this marriage doesn't last, I'm going to kill both of them!

HERMAN: Well, as long as we're all stuck up here running around in circles like a bunch of cats chasing their tails, can I interest anyone in a game of poker?

(Takes a deck of cards out of his coat pocket.)

JACK: Why not? Nothing else to do. Come on, Liz, trade places with him so we can kill some time up here.

LIZ: OK, but no betting.

JACK: No betting? You gamble with our lives on this god-forsaken plane, and you tell *me* no betting?

LIZ: All right, all right, go ahead.

(LIZ and HERMAN trade places and HERMAN and JACK start playing cards.)

JACK: Do you always carry a deck of cards with you?

HERMAN: Yep. You know what they say – "Unlucky in love ..."

JACK: Maybe it's your clothes.

HERMAN: What's wrong with my clothes?

JACK: Nobody dresses like that anymore, except maybe Wayne Newton!

HERMAN: Well anyway, once in a while Lady Luck is good to me.

JACK: Well, let's see who's side she's on tonight.

LIZ: How are you doing, honey? Still nervous?

JENNIFER: Not really. I can't explain it, but for some reason the fear is gone. I'm actually relaxed.

LIZ: Maybe it's because we're having such a smooth and comfortable ride.

JENNIFER: Yeah, that must be it.

JACK: Hey, when are you going to land this thing? My watch seems to have stopped, but it feels like we've been circling for hours.

LIZ: Yeah, doesn't this plane ever run out of gas?

PILOT: You don't get it, do you? None of you – you still don't get it.

LIZ: Get what?

PILOT: Think about it, Liz. You seem to be the smartest one here. A while back, I thought you almost had it.

LIZ: Had what?

PILOT: This plane is not going to land. This aircraft made its final landing five years ago, just east of New London.

LIZ: What? You're crazy! Besides, the airport is in New London.

PILOT: *(Holds up first two fingers)* Missed it by that much.

JENNIFER: But there's nothing east of New London –
except the Atlantic Ocean.
PILOT: Bingo!

(Pause)

LIZ: Who were the passengers on board that night?
PILOT: Don't any of you look familiar to each other?
LIZ: Well yes, in fact, I was telling Jennifer before we
boarded that she looked familiar to me. And now that you
mention it, I have experienced deja vu more than once tonight.
ALL: Yeah, me too.
PILOT: That's because, as deja vu indicates, you've done
this before. We've all done this before – five times before to
be exact.
JENNIFER: When?
PILOT: Every August 15th for the last five years.
HERMAN: Where are we going?
PILOT: Nowhere. We are caught in an eternal loop – the
ultimate Bermuda Triangle.
HERMAN: How do we get out of it?
PILOT: Now if I knew the answer to that, would I be
here?

*(Takes an apron out from somewhere in the cockpit and puts
      it on. Gets out a bottle of Champaign and some glasses.)*

HERMAN: I guess not.

(Pause)

JACK: Are you telling us that we're dead, and that we've
been dead for five years?

PILOT: Now you're catching on!

JACK: You're nuts!

LIZ: You know, you really shouldn't make jokes like that – especially when you've got people on board who are afraid of flying.

JENNIFER: Yeah, really.

PILOT: I hate to be the bearer of bad news, but this is no joke.

JACK: Do you mean to tell me that we will be taking this same flight over and over again for all eternity?

PILOT: *(Pops the cork of the Champaign)* Every August 15th.

LIZ: Why? What did we ever do to deserve this?

JACK: What do we do the other 364 days of the year?

HERMAN: Why didn't we just get killed and die? Ever hear of rest in peace?

JENNIFER: How come I don't feel dead?

ALL: Feel dead?

JENNIFER: You know what I mean.

LIZ: Yeah, I know. *(To PILOT)* Does this happen to everybody when they die, or just us lucky ones who get sentenced to a hell of repeating their untimely deaths annually for all eternity?

JENNIFER: Tell us! Tell us now! What's going on?

PILOT: Hey, don't ask me. Who do I look like, God?

LIZ: That's another thing. Who are you? How come you knew we were dead and we didn't?

PILOT: Because I'm the Captain.

JENNIFER: No really, how did you know?

PILOT: I don't know. I just did. I guess one of us had to know, and since I'm at the controls, I had to know where we were going – or at least where we were not going.

HERMAN: So you really don't know where we're headed?

PILOT: No. My job is to get us up in the air and that's it. Once we're up here, it's out of my hands.

LIZ: You know, I'm always the first to try to make the best of a bad situation, but this is a tough one. Well, "If I must die, I will encounter darkness as a bride and hug it in my arms."

JACK: What?

LIZ: "If I must die, I will encounter darkness as a bride and hug it in my arms."

JACK: What's that supposed to mean?

LIZ: I guess we might as well accept our deaths and make the best of it.

JACK: Who'd you get that crazy idea from?

LIZ: Shakespeare.

JACK: I should have known. Whenever I can't understand what she's saying, she's quoting Shakespeare.

LIZ: And what's wrong with Shakespeare?

JACK: He talks funny.

LIZ: Look, just because you don't understand him, don't try to make *him* out to be the dummy.

JACK: Well, what does he know? He's been dead for 500 years.

LIZ: Well then, he must know what he's talking about.

JENNIFER: I like, "Because I could not stop for Death, He kindly stopped for me. The carriage held but just ourselves and immortality."

HERMAN: Who said that?

JENNIFER: Emily Dickensen.

LIZ: She's one of my favorites.

JENNIFER: Mine too.

JACK: How about, "Death sucks!"

LIZ: Who, pray tell, said that?

JACK: I did.

JENNIFER: I'll drink to that!

LIZ: Oh, honey, don't encourage him. He couldn't quote literature if his life depended on it.

JACK: Don't have to worry about that anymore, do I? Besides, I read a book once.

HERMAN: Yeah? What was it?

JACK: "Fear Strikes Out."

LIZ: Oh great – a 30 year old book about a wacko baseball player who used to throw tomatoes at the umpire from the stands when he was called out and ran around the bases backwards when he hit a homerun – literature at its best!

JACK: You're such a snob! Something has to be totally un-understandable before you consider it literature.

LIZ: Well, anyway, enough of this. Let's get back to the situation at hand. *(To PILOT)* You must know more than you're telling us.

PILOT: I do, but I've been sworn to secrecy.

JENNIFER: By who?

PILOT: I can't tell you that either. You'll find out soon enough.

JENNIFER: I want to know what's going on, right now!

PILOT: All in good time, my pretty, all in good time.

HERMAN: Just tell us this much. We're not really just circling endlessly, are we? We're actually headed somewhere, right?

PILOT: That's right.

LIZ: Is it Heaven or Hell?

PILOT: Yes.

LIZ: Well, which one?

JACK: Oh, come on, Liz. Do you think this is how they'd bring us to Heaven?

LIZ: But why? I mean, why would we go to Hell? We've always been good people.

PILOT: How many times do you think they've heard that one?

LIZ: But what are we doing? Why are we here?

JENNIFER: Maybe we're supposed to stay on this plane until we figure out why we were sent to Hell instead of Heaven. That could be part of the agony – figuring out and admitting why we were bad enough on earth to be damned for all eternity.

PILOT: Very good!

LIZ: Well, I don't like it.

PILOT: I haven't met anyone who enjoyed Hell.

HERMAN: OK, let me get this straight. We have to keep repeating this flight over and over again until we know what we did wrong while we were alive, and then we can begin to serve out time in Hell?

PILOT: That's right.

JACK: Well, maybe we're better off just staying on board the plane. I mean, I don't like it, but it seems like Hell would be a Hell of a lot worse than this.

JENNIFER: Yeah, I agree. This isn't as bad as I thought it was going to be.

PILOT: Don't be fooled by the temporarily smooth ride. This is the calm before the storm. Don't forget; if you don't come to terms with your demise this time around, you still have the crash into the Atlantic Ocean to repeat, and believe me, none of you wants to go through that again! We all have to face it sooner or later.

LIZ: OK, who wants to start?

HERMAN: *(To PILOT)* Why don't you go first?

PILOT: I've already done my part. This was my sentence – to spend eternity bringing condemned souls to their final destination and having to stay with them until they're ready to be delivered, reliving their deaths with them.

JACK: Wow! That's the pits!

PILOT: No kidding! OK, let's get this show on the road. Since you've come this far finally, I guess it won't hurt for me to give you a little hint as to what is expected. You're all familiar with the Ten Commandments?

JACK: I saw the movie once, but that was a long time ago.

PILOT: Everybody think back. What was your sin? Jennifer, why don't we start with you?

JENNIFER: Well, I stole a candy bar from a grocery store once when I was seven.

PILOT: I don't think that would do it. Think harder. What's the worst thing you've ever done?

JENNIFER: You mean like the time I posed for that photographer?

PILOT: Yeah, like that.

JENNIFER: Well, I needed the money. All my friends were taking a cruise to Europe and I wanted to go with them.

PILOT: No excuses, just stick to the facts.

JENNIFER: Well, is that it?

PILOT: You tell me.

JENNIFER: That's the worst thing I've ever done – unless, does sex count?

PILOT: Everything counts.

JENNIFER: OK, so I was a little promiscuous.

PILOT: A little?

JENNIFER: Well, who isn't these days?

PILOT: Indeed! *(Turns to HERMAN)* Herman?

JACK: He should go to Hell just for the way he dresses!

LIZ: If I were you, I wouldn't throw any stones right now.

JACK: OK, OK.

HERMAN: When I was a little kid, I was a real nerd. I was so good, I made everybody sick.

PILOT: What about when you grew up?

HERMAN: Well, I gambled a little, but not that often, and never any serious betting – just a friendly game of poker now and then.

PILOT: You have a pretty good poker face, don't you, Herman?

HERMAN: Not bad.

PILOT: Good enough to use in your business? Is that how you sold so many bogus life insurance policies?

HERMAN: You know about that, huh?

PILOT: *(Takes three playing cards out of HERMAN's shirt pocket)* We know about everything, Herman.

HERMAN: Well, I only did that to little old ladies who were alone and didn't have very long to live anyway. What else were they going to spend their money on?

JENNIFER: I'm sure they all had better things to spend their money on than a scam!

HERMAN: OK, so I blew it. At least I wasn't a slut!

JENNIFER: No, you were just a schmuck!

PILOT: What about Jack?

LIZ: Book him, Dano!

JACK: Look who's talking!

LIZ: Everybody get comfortable. This one's going to take a while.

JACK: Hey, take your pick! I pulverized just about every commandment in the book, but who didn't. I mean, I didn't break all of them. I never killed anybody, except during the war, and that doesn't count. I was only following orders, and besides, they were Nazis, so they didn't deserve to live anyway. I never stole anything or cheated anybody like old Herman over there. Income taxes don't count, do they? Nah – that's just the government, and that's the biggest bunch of crooks on earth. They took too much from me, so I took it back from them, any way I could. It was my money, so you can't really call that stealing. Let's see, what else? I don't know. I guess that's it. So if they want to send me to Hell for screwing the government and knocking off a few Nazis, let them. *(To LIZ)* OK, Mother Theresa, it's your turn.

LIZ: Hey, I'm not perfect. I know that. But I certainly never expected this. It's probably guilt by association.

(Points to JACK.)

JACK: Yeah, misery loves company. Come on Liz, the rest of us have leveled with each other. Think of it this way – what have you got to lose?

LIZ: That's true, but I honestly can't think of anything I ever did that was so terrible. I know I wasn't perfect, but I really don't know why I'm here.

PILOT: Does the name Pancho Villa ring a bell?

LIZ: Oh, come on. That was a terrible, terrible thing, but it was an accident.

JACK: An accident?

LIZ: Yes! I didn't know it was going to kill him. I loved that dog!

JENNIFER: What did you do?

LIZ: About ten years ago. we had a toy poodle named Pancho Villa. One summer day, I gave him a bath just before we were leaving to go to New York for the weekend. I didn't want to leave him all wet, and towel drying him just didn't do the job well enough. Well, we had just gotten our first microwave oven.

JENNIFER: Oh, God! Oh, my God!

LIZ: Well, I didn't know!

JENNIFER: How long?

LIZ: Three minutes.

JENNIFER: Oh my God! How could you?

HERMAN: What happened?

(JACK makes a noise like a bomb exploding.)

JENNIFER: He blew up?

JACK: Like a cherry bomb on the fourth of July.

JENNIFER: Oh God! You know, I heard about that happening to someone, but I didn't believe it. I thought it was just an old wive's tale.

JACK: It was, and this is the old wife who did it.

LIZ: I lived with that nightmare for the rest of my life.

JACK: It ain't over yet, Babe.

JENNIFER: I hate to tell you, but I'd send you to Hell for that too.

LIZ: Yeah, I guess I would too. *(TO PILOT)* Well, there you have it. We've all aired our dirty laundry. Now what?

PILOT: Well, well, well – what a bunch of pathetic, disgusting degenerates! You're all certainly headed for the right place. Congratulations, sinners, you did it. Now for the part you have all been waiting for. We have just started our final descent to your final destination. Ladies and gentlemen, welcome to Hell!

END OF PLAY

SCENE ONE

Set Props:
> Cleaning Cloth
> Microphone for Agent
> One Oxygen Mask
> Apron
> Bottle of Champagne
> Five Champagne Glasses

Hand Props:
> Newspaper
> Two Small Suitcases
> Four Airline Tickets
> Business Cards
> Barf Bag
> Index Card
> Deck of Cards

SCENE TWO

Set Props:
> One Oxygen Mask
> Apron
> Bottle of Champagne
> Five Champagne Glasses

Hand Props:
> Index Card
> Deck of Cards

Costumes: AGENT: Black Suit with White Carnation
> HERMAN: Plaid Suit with Bow Tie
> JACK: Old "Live-In" Sweater, Slacks & Shirt, Watch
> LIZ: Pants and Blouse
> JENNIFER: Jeans and Shirt
> PILOT: Pilot's Uniform

**ON HOLD AT
30,000 FEET**

.

CHARACTERS

HARVEY:
  30's-40's, Extremely Nervous

DAVID:
  30's-40's, Distant, Unfriendly

FLIGHT ATTENDANTS #1 & #2:
  20's-30's

PILOT:
  Voice Over

TIME

Approximately 30 Minutes

SETTING

On Board an Airplane

Scene One

*(HARVEY enters. He's wearing an overcoat with a crucifix, a
Star of David, a scapular. a Buddha charm [Ho Tai], a
rosary, a silver talisman, and a St. Christopher's medal
around his neck; two bracelets; and a four-leaf clover
under his coat. DAVID is sitting in the window seat
reading a book. HARVEY puts a towel on the seat and
head rest before he sits down. DAVID watches him do
this. He looks at HARVEY then goes back to reading his
book.)*

HARVEY: I don't know who's been sitting in that seat.
I'm not a fanatic. I'm just cautious. *(DAVID doesn't respond)*
*(Looks up at the buttons above him. Feels the air coming out
of the air button)* Where is this air coming from?

DAVID: You're asking me where air comes from?

HARVEY: Not all air, just this air.

DAVID: I don't know. Ask the Flight Attendant.

HARVEY: *(Looks in the aisle and calls)* Excuse me.
Excuse me.

DAVID: Push the call button.

HARVEY: The what?

*(DAVID pushes the call button above HARVEY's seat.
FLIGHT ATTENDANT #1 enters.)*

FLIGHT ATTENDANT #1: Yes sir?

HARVEY: Where is this air coming from?

FLIGHT ATTENDANT #1: From our air conditioning system. Don't worry. It's clean, fresh air.

HARVEY: I can imagine how clean it is. However, my concern right now is how is it getting in here?

DAVID: Tell him about the little holes in the plane above everyone's seats.

FLIGHT ATTENDANT #1: Sir, there are no holes in the aircraft. *(To HARVEY)* You have nothing to worry about. Our air conditioning is just like the kind you have in your car. It's perfectly safe. Enjoy the flight, Sir.

(Exits)

HARVEY: This is my first flight.

DAVID: I can tell.

HARVEY: *(Takes off his coat)* But that's OK. I'm prepared.

DAVID: My God! You look like a jewelry exhibit from the '70s. What is all this?

HARVEY: This is a crucifix. This is a Star of David. This is a scapular. This is a four leaf clover. This is a charm bracelet with shells. This is ...

DAVID: *(Holds up his hand for HARVEY to stop)* Sorry I asked. Superstitious?

HARVEY: I just want to cover all the bases. This is my first time flying and I'm a little nervous.

DAVID: The metal detector must have blown a fuse when you walked through.

HARVEY: That was quite a spectacle.

DAVID: I'll bet.

HARVEY: I'm used to it.

DAVID: I'll bet. *(Pause)* What's that smell?

HARVEY: That's my garlic necklace.

(Takes it out from under his shirt.)

DAVID: Are you expecting Dracula?

HARVEY: It's just for luck.

DAVID: You're going to have the whole airplane smelling like an Italian deli.

HARVEY: You don't like Italian food?

DAVID: I love Italian food, but I wouldn't wear garlic cologne.

(HARVEY looks around nervously.)

HARVEY: Oh good Lord! We're moving.

DAVID: You didn't pay $200 to sit at the gate, did you?

HARVEY: Of course not. I just didn't expect to move so soon.

DAVID: The sooner we move, the sooner we stop.

HARVEY: That's a good way to look at it. That's a very good way to look at it. *(Quietly to himself)* The sooner we move the sooner we stop. The sooner we move the sooner we stop.

(HARVEY blesses himself and folds his hands. About 5 seconds later he folds his arms and sits as if he's meditating. About 5 seconds later he puts his arms on the arm rests and says a mantra. About 5 seconds later he takes the rabbit's foot out of his pocket and rubs it. About 5 seconds later, he rubs his Ho Tai.)

DAVID: Can't decide who to pray to?

HARVEY: Please, don't talk to me until we're *(Pause)* you know.

DAVID: *(Whispers)* Up in the air?

HARVEY: Shh!

DAVID: *(Laughs)* You're gonna be a lot of fun when we take off.

HARVEY: Shh!

(Pause)

DAVID: You're really scared, aren't you?

HARVEY: I've sat on an airplane four times and gotten off at the last minute just before they shut the door each time. This is the first time I've stayed on.

DAVID: I'm sure you've heard that it's safer to fly in a plane than it is to ride in a car.

HARVEY: Of course.

DAVID: Do you ride in cars?

HARVEY: Yes.

DAVID: Then why are you more afraid of something that's less dangerous?

HARVEY: Because I don't believe that.

DAVID: Statistics have proven it.

HARVEY: Screw statistics. Statistics don't fly 20,000 feet in the air.

DAVID: 25,000 feet.

HARVEY: Thank you very much.

DAVID: Look, why don't you just sit there and pray quietly. You've got enough saints and gods and good luck charms to take you all the way to London.

(FLIGHT ATTENDANT #1 enters and stands in the aisle as

the voice of FLIGHT ATTENDANT #2 is heard over a loud speaker off stage.)

FLIGHT ATTENDANT #2: Good afternoon, ladies and gentlemen, and welcome to Coastal Airlines, Flight 437, non-stop service to Los Angeles. Please make sure that your seat belts are securely fastened, and that your seat backs and tray tables are in the up-right position. This is a non-smoking flight. No smoking is permitted anywhere in the aircraft, including the lavatories.

HARVEY: No smoking? Are you kidding?

FLIGHT ATTENDANT #2: *(Over loud speaker)* No, Sir, I am not kidding.

HARVEY: Oh, good Lord!

DAVID: Don't interrupt her.

HARVEY: *(To FLIGHT ATTENDANT)* Sorry. *(TO DAVID)* I can't go an hour without smoking.

DAVID: You'll live.

FLIGHT ATTENDANT #3: No smoking is permitted anywhere in the aircraft, including the lavatories. Please direct your attention to the Flight Attendant in the aisle. To fasten the seat belt, insert the strap into the buckle. To unfasten the seat belt, lift up on the metal handle.

HARVEY: *(Struggling with his seat belt, says to FLIGHT ATTENDANT)* What buckle? Where?

(FLIGHT ATTENDANT #1 holds up her hand for FLIGHT ATTENDANT #2 to stop talking, then goes over to HARVEY and fastens his seat belt for him, then returns to the aisle.)

DAVID: *(TO FLIGHT ATTENDANT #1)* He's not with me.

(FLIGHT ATTENDANT #2 peaks out from behind the curtain and looks at HARVEY, then looks at FLIGHT ATTENDANT #1 and continues.)

FLIGHT ATTENDANT #2: After take-off, the Captain will turn off the "Fasten Seat Belt" sign, but it is recommended ...

HARVEY: *(To FLIGHT ATTENDANT #1)* I just got it on. I am not taking this seat belt off until we have landed and the plane has stopped.

FLIGHT ATTENDANT #2: *(Over microphone – speaking slowly)* You do not have to take the seat belt off. The sign is turned off so you can remove the seat belt if you want to.

HARVEY: I don't want to.

FLIGHT ATTENDANT #2: Then don't! *(Returns to her "speech voice")* Please familiarize yourself with the safety instructions located in the seat pocket in front of you.

(FLIGHT ATTENDANT #1 holds up a safety instruction card.)

HARVEY: *(To FLIGHT ATTENDANT #1)* Can I see that? *(FLIGHT ATTENDANT #1 holds up her hand to FLIGHT ATTENDANT #2 to stop. Comes over to HARVEY and finds the safety instructions in his seat pocket and hands it to him)* What is all this? Are these all the things that can go wrong? Why are there so many safety precautions?

FLIGHT ATTENDANT #1: That's all they are, sir, just precautions. Enjoy the flight.

(Returns to the aisle and signals to FLIGHT ATTENDANT #2 to continue.)

FLIGHT ATTENDANT #2: *(Over microphone)* The emergency exits are located at the front and the back of the aircraft.

(FLIGHT ATTENDANT #1 points to the emergency exits. HARVEY takes off his seat belt and stands up. He points to where the FLIGHT ATTENDANT pointed and starts to go into the aisle.)

FLIGHT ATTENDANT #1: *(Rushes over to HARVEY from the aisle)* Sir, please be seated and buckle your seat belt.

HARVEY: I want to see where the emergency exits are.

FLIGHT ATTENDANT #1: I'll show you when the "Fasten Seat Belt" sign has been turned off. For now, please remain seated and fasten your seat belt.

FLIGHT ATTENDANT #2: *(Enters holding the microphone)* I'll be happy to show you where the exits are once we get in the air.

DAVID: Let me show him. I'll even show him how they work. *(To HARVEY)* Now shut up and let them finish.

(FLIGHT ATTENDANT #1 returns to the aisle. FLIGHT ATTENDANT #2 stands next to her with the microphone.)

FLIGHT ATTENDANT #2: *(Says to FLIGHT ATTENDANT #1)* I might as well stay out here. We're never going to finish this anyway. *(Into microphone)* In the event of an emergency, your seat cushions can be used as a flotation device.

HARVEY: Flotation devise? What is this – the Titanic in the sky? You tell that pilot to stay away from the water. Keep this airplane in the sky and we won't have to worry about flotation devices.

FLIGHT ATTENDANT #2: *(Looking at HARVEY and smiling)* If there is a sudden change n the cabin pressure, oxygen masks will drop from overhead. *(Knocks FLIGHT ATTENDANT #1 with her elbow to direct her attention to HARVEY as FLIGHT ATTENDANT #1 demonstrates the oxygen mask. Both FLIGHT ATTENDANTS watch HARVEY's reaction to what is being said)* Place the mask over your nose and mouth and breathe normally. *(FLIGHT ATTENDANT #2 looks at DAVID as she continues)* If you are traveling with a child, secure your oxygen mask before helping him with his.

DAVID: I told you. He's not with me!

FLIGHT ATTENDANT #2: We will be serving beverages for your enjoyment momentarily.

HARVEY: *(To FLIGHT ATTENDANTS)* None for me. I don't want anything to eat or drink. I have a very sensitive stomach and ...

FLIGHT ATTENDANT #2: I give up. *(Into microphone)* Everybody just stay seated. Nobody move, and we'll all get along just fine.

(Exits)

DAVID: Now look what you've done. Happy?
HARVEY: I'll talk to her.
DAVID: No! Just leave the poor girl alone.
HARVEY: I know. I'll do my breathing exercises.
DAVID: Fine. Just sit there and breathe.

(HARVEY sits perfectly still for about 30 seconds. DAVID

looks over at him curiously. HARVEY notices DAVID staring at him.)

HARVEY: What?

DAVID: Nothing.

HARVEY: Why are you staring at me?

DAVID: You said you were going to do some breathing exercises.

HARVEY: I was doing them.

DAVID: You weren't doing anything.

HARVEY: I was doing my stress exercises. All you do is breathe in one nostril and out the other.

DAVID: *(Tries to imitate what HARVEY is doing)* Don't you have to plug one side of your nose to do that?

HARVEY: You don't plug one side of your nose. You don't touch or move your nose at all.

DAVID: *(Trying to do this, but is moving his nose)* You can't block off one side of your nose without touching or moving it. That's physically impossible.

HARVEY: This is not a physical exercise. It's done with your mind and is meant to relieve stress.

DAVID: It's done with your mind?

HARVEY: Yes.

DAVID: That's my kind of exercise.

HARVEY: It's mind over matter. You breathe in one nostril and out the other eight times. Then you reverse the process. It's very relaxing. You should try it.

DAVID: That's OK. When I want to relax I'll stick to my old friend, Jack Daniel's.

HARVEY: What happening? Why are we going so fast? He shouldn't be going so fast while we're still on the ground!

DAVID: Don't worry. The pilot won't get a ticket. He knows the speed limit.

HARVEY: Oh good Lord!

(Puts his head between his knees.)

DAVID: I had a feeling you were going to enjoy take off.

(HARVEY begins taking deep breaths. Suddenly he starts hyperventilating.)

HARVEY: *(While hyperventilating)* I'm going to have a heart attack! Bag! Paper bag!

DAVID: *(Takes a barf bag out of the seat pocket in from of him and hands it to HARVEY)* Here.

(HARVEY breaths into the bag a few times.)

HARVEY: Thank you. I'm glad to see the airlines is prepared for passengers who hyperventilate. See? There must be lots of people in my situation or these bags would not be here.

DAVID: That's a barf bag.

HARVEY: A what?

DAVID: A barf bag. That's not for people who hyperventilate. It's for people who throw up.

HARVEY: People who throw up?

DAVID: Sure. You've got one too.

(HARVEY looks in his seat pocket and takes out the barf bag.)

HARVEY: Great. Everybody's going to throw up. I hate throwing up. I don't want to throw up.

DAVID: Would you relax. You're not going to throw up.

HARVEY: How do you know?

DAVID: Because if you do, I'll kill you.

HARVEY: I wish Dr. Panelli was here.

DAVID: Doctor? You sick?

(Worried more about being bothered by someone who's sick than he is about HARVEY's health.)

HARVEY: He's my Analyst.

DAVID: I should have known.

HARVEY: He could get me through this. If only I could talk to him.

DAVID: *(Points to the phone on the seat in front of HARVEY)* Call him.

HARVEY: Call him? Oh my God! A phone. Oh, thank God. How does it work?

DAVID: Do you have a phone card?

HARVEY: Yes.

DAVID: Put it in here and follow the instructions.

(HARVEY takes a credit card out of his wallet, puts it in the slot by the phone, and dials a number.)

HARVEY: Janet, let me speak to Dr. Panelli. *(Pause)* Yes, it's me. *(Pause)* No, I didn't get off the plane again. That's where I'm calling from. *(Pause – to DAVID)* I'm on hold.

PILOT: *(PILOT's voice is heard from off stage)* Good afternoon, ladies and gentlemen. This is your captain speaking. My name is Captain Jerry Harrison, and I would like to welcome you aboard Coastal Airlines, flight 437. We anticipate a smooth ride to Los Angeles today with mild tail winds and will be flying at an altitude of 30,000 feet.

HARVEY: 30,000 feet? Don't you dare take this plane up 30,000 feet.

PILOT: I'm sorry, but that's our scheduled altitude for the flight.

HARVEY: I don't care what your scheduled altitude is. You are not to take this plane up over 25,000 feet. Do you hear me?

PILOT: Excuse me, but who's the pilot here?

HARVEY: I am the customer and the customer's always right!

PILOT: Would you like to come up and fly the plane, Sir?

HARVEY: What I would like is for you to keep this plane at a normal height. In fact, I demand that you do not take this plane over 25,000 feet! You got that?

PILOT: I got that.

DAVID: I can see it now. You're not going to live through this flight.

PILOT: We will be flying at an altitude of 30,000 feet. Our flying time is estimated at one hour and five minutes. No smoking is permitted in any part of the aircraft, including the lavatories. I will turn off the "Fasten Seat Belt" sign shortly and the Flight Attendants will provide you with beverages for your enjoyment.

HARVEY: Enjoyment? The only enjoyment I'm going to get out of this flight is when it's over. Now stop jabbering and pay attention to where we're going. You got that?

PILOT: Don't make me come out there! *(Pause)* Have a pleasant flight and thank you for choosing Coastal Airlines.

HARVEY: **30**,000 feet! We're going to be flying at 30,000 feet!

DAVID: Twenty-five, thirty – what's the difference?

HARVEY: Almost a mile. *(Into the phone)* Janet? Where is he? How long is he going to be on the phone? *(Pause)* Well, could you slip him a note telling him I'm waiting to talk to him? *(Pause)* No, he can't call me tonight at the hotel. What good will that do me? I need him now. I'm 30,000 feet in the air. *(To DAVID)* I must be out of my mind.

DAVID: Must be.

HARVEY: *(To DAVID)* This is ridiculous. He's always there when I need him, and now when I need him the most, he's yapping to some nut case.

DAVID: *(Laughs)* Isn't that kind of like the pot calling the kettle black?

HARVEY: I'm not a nut case. I'm just afraid of flying. Actually, I'm not afraid of flying. I'm afraid of crashing. And what normal person wouldn't be?

DAVID: If you'd stop harping on it all the time, maybe you wouldn't be so scared. While you're on hold, why don't you try thinking about something else.

HARVEY: Like what?

DAVID: I don't know. Do you have a family?

HARVEY: No.

DAVID: Girl friend?

HARVEY: No. I did – up until a month ago.

DAVID: What happened?

HARVEY: Remember when I told you that I've gotten off airplanes four times before they took off?

DAVID: Yeah.

HARVEY: The first time was a business trip for a company I used to work for. I got fired because I lost an account when I missed the meeting I was supposed to go to. The other three times were vacations that she and I were supposed to take.

DAVID: I don't blame her. I'd dump you too.
HARVEY: Thanks for understanding.
DAVID: I do understand. You're a neurotic mess.
HARVEY: I can't help it. I was toilet trained too early.
DAVID: Did your shrink tell you that?
HARVEY: Yes, and he's right. I remember.
DAVID: You remember?
HARVEY: Sort of – when I think about it hard enough.

(Looks like he's concentrating.)

DAVID: Don't hurt your brain.
FLIGHT ATTENDANT #2: *(Enters with a cart of drinks and says to DAVID)* Would you like a drink, Sir?
DAVID: Whiskey, straight up.
FLIGHT ATTENDANT #2: *(Fixes DAVID a drink and hands it to him with a bag of peanuts)* That'll be $3.00 please. *(DAVID hands the FLIGHT ATTENDANT $3.00)* Thank you, Sir. *(To HARVEY)* Would you like a drink?
HARVEY: No, thank you.
DAVID: Go ahead. It'll help you relax.
HARVEY: No. I don't want anything to eat or drink. My stomach gets upset very easily. *(Into the phone)* Dr. Panelli? Hello? *(FLIGHT ATTENDANT #2 exits)* Yes. Yes, it's me, Harvey. *(Pause)* I'm not doing well at all, doctor. You have to talk me through this. *(Pause)* What do you mean you're busy? I don't care who you've got on the other line. Just because he's the Mayor doesn't mean he comes first. I'm just as important as he is, and I pay you just as much as he does. *(Pause)* Well, I'm going to have a heart attack if you don't talk me through this. *(Pause)* Oh, all right, put me on hold again, but hurry back. *(To DAVID)* He's got someone on another line. I can't tell you who it is, but he's a big baby.

DAVID: Is he charging you for this call?

HARVEY: Of course.

DAVID: So shrinks charge you for phone calls just like lawyers do, huh?

HARVEY: Oh yes, but he's worth it. Too bad I can't just add it to my expense report. Hey, I could organize that while I'm waiting for him to come back. That's something that could keep my mind occupied.

(Gets paper, a pen, and a calculator out of a brief case.)

DAVID: But you haven't even taken the trip yet. How do you know what your expenses are going to be?

HARVEY: I have it all figured out. *(Writes as he speaks)* The hotel is $120.00 a night, so two nights would be $240.00 plus tax makes that $260.40. The car rental is $29.00 a day, so for two days that's *(The bell is heard as the "Fasten Seat Belt" sign goes off)* What was that?

DAVID: The pilot just turned of the "Fasten Seat Belt" sign.

HARVEY: Well, he can take his seat belt off if he wants to, but I'm keeping mine on. *(Into the phone)* Dr. Panelli? Where have you been? *(Pause)* Oh, who cares about that crook? He's just a big baby anyway. *(Pause)* No, I will not hold on again. I won't. I won't. I won't. *(To DAVID)* This is ridiculous! I'll show him. *(Slams the phone down)* Oh, good Lord, what have I done?

DAVID: Hey, it's OK. You don't need him to talk you through the flight.

HARVEY: Yes I do.

DAVID: No you don't. You'll be fine. Go back to your expense report.

HARVEY: I can't. I'm too nervous.

DAVID: You were doing it before.

HARVEY: That was when Dr. Panelli was on the phone.

DAVID: He wasn't on the phone. You were on hold. You weren't even talking to him.

HARVEY: I know, but he was there in spirit. *(HARVEY and DAVID jump slightly in their seats) (Screams)* What was that? *(Pushes the Call Button repeatedly)* What was that? Call 911! I'll call them.

(Picks up the phone.)

FLIGHT ATTENDANT #1: Yes, Sir?

HARVEY: What was that? What did we hit?

FLIGHT ATTENDANT #1: We didn't hit anything, Sir. That was just a small air pocket.

HARVEY: *(Hangs up the phone)* Why did the plane jerk like that?

FLIGHT ATTENDANT #1: Don't worry, Sir. It's all over and we're perfectly safe. Enjoy the flight.

HARVEY: If she tells me to enjoy the flight one more time, I'm going to slap her. *(DAVID puts his seat back and closes his eyes)* What are you doing?

DAVID: Taking a nap. Is that all right with you?

HARVEY: But I need someone to talk to.

DAVID: Look, I don't even know you. I'm not responsible for getting you through this flight. I'm a little tired and I would like to take a nap. I don't care if you sit there and talk to yourself. Just don't talk to me.

(Lies back and shuts his eyes.)

HARVEY: *(To himself)* I can't talk to myself. People will think I'm crazy. But then, people on soap operas talk to themselves all the time and nobody thinks they're crazy. Yeah, John and Kristin are always talking to themselves and they're two of the most respected people in Salem. But I can't help myself. I don't know what to say to make myself feel better. I need to talk to someone who can make me feel safe. I know.

(Pushes the Call Button.)
(The two FLIGHT ATTENDANTS are seen beyond a curtain flipping a coin.)

FLIGHT ATTENDANT #2: Damn! *(Enters)* Yes, Sir?
HARVEY: I didn't want you. I wanted the other Flight Attendant.
FLIGHT ATTENDANT #2: Well, I lost and you got me. *(HARVEY doesn't say anything)* I'll be happy to take you to the emergency exit now if you'd like to go.
HARVEY: No. I want to talk to the other Flight Attendant.
FLIGHT ATTENDANT #2: I'll go get her.

(Exits. FLIGHT ATTENDANT #1 enters laughing.)

HARVEY: Could you stay here and talk to me?
FLIGHT ATTENDANT #1: I'd love to, Sir, but I'm very busy.
HARVEY: Oh, everybody's busy. Please? Just for a little while?
FLIGHT ATTENDANT #1: I really don't have the time, Sir. It won't be long before we land. Don't worry. You're

doing just fine. *(Hands him a pillow)* Try to rest a little. Enjoy the flight.

HARVEY: *(Screams into the pillow) (Yells to FLIGHT ATTENDANT #1 in the aisle)* If I was enjoying the flight, I wouldn't need someone to talk to. *(Looks around to see if anyone heard him)* I know. I'll call The Psychic Center. Madam Kiki will tell me that the plane is going to land safely and then I'll know for sure, and I'll be fine. *(Takes his phone card out again and places another call. As he dials, he says the number out loud)* 1-900-976-SCAM. *(Pause)* Hello, Madam Kiki? Thank God you're there. This is Harvey. *(Pause)* I'm sorry. Of course you knew. I need your help. *(Pause)* I'm in an airplane. *(Pause)* That's it. *(Pause)* Yes, that's the problem. *(Pause)* It's a problem because I'm sitting in a seat on this thing with total strangers *(Looking at DAVID)* who are no help at all, and our lives are depending on a hostile pilot with psychotic flight attendants. Worse yet, I'm in a gigantic machine 30,000 feet in the air, not to mention the weather, which nobody has any control over. *(Pause)* No, the weather's fine, but that could change any minute. You know California weather. And we did just hit an air pocket, whatever the Hell that is. *(Pause)* But I feel so helpless. There's nothing I can do but sit here. My fate is completely out of my control. *(Pause)* What? Wait! No! I will not hol ...

DAVID: She put you on hold, huh? Do you really believe in those psychos?

HARVEY: *Psychics.* And yes, I do.

DAVID: You're nuttier than a fruit cake, you know that?

HARVEY: That's a very cruel thing for you to say. I just need a little help, that's all. Life is very tough, especially when you live in a big city. Bit cities are very stressful.

DAVID: Then why do you live in a big city?

HARVEY: I was born and raised in San Francisco. I guess I'm used to it.

DAVID: Apparently not.

HARVEY: Sometimes I think I am. I mean usually I love living in the City, but there are times when I'm tempted to move up north to a small town. Petersville would be nice.

DAVID: Petersville?

HARVEY: Yes. I friend of mine was in a play up in Petersville once and I went to see it. It's a very nice little town.

DAVID: I used to have to go to Petersville on business once in a while and spend two or three days there at a time. I've never been to a more boring town in my life.

HARVEY: You're probably confusing boring with quiet. I bet there's a lot to do in Petersville.

DAVID: Let me put it this way. If you move to Petersville, when you wake up in the morning, whatever you do, don't look out your window.

HARVEY: Why not?

DAVID: Cause then you won't have anything to do in the afternoon.

HARVEY: Very funny. *(Into the phone)* Madam Kiki? I'm so glad you're back. I need you to tell me that this plane is going to land safely and I'm going to be alright. *(Pause)* I know, but I need to hear it again. *(Pause)* Can't you just tap into your inner soul and see it? *(Pause)* Oh, please? I'm going to have a heart attack if somebody doesn't talk to me soon. *(Pause)* Sure. Why not?

DAVID: Where'd she go, to consult her Oujia Board?

HARVEY: No. She's reading tea leaves.

DAVID: You mean she's having a cup of tea.

HARVEY: No. She's reading tea leaves, and she's going to come back and tell me that the plane will land safely, I'm going to be just fine, and I will never be afraid of flying again. And she'll be right.

DAVID: Man, what color is the sky in your world?

HARVEY: Go ahead and make fun if you want. I have great faith n Madam Kiki. She told me my past perfectly the first time we met, and everything she's predicted for my future has come true.

DAVID: Like what?

HARVEY: She predicted my breakup with Tina; she predicted that the next time I got on a plane I would stay on; and she predicted that by the end of the flight I will be resting very peacefully, and I'm sure that once she comes back to the phone and tells me that the plane will be landing safely, that I'll be just fine, and once again her prediction will come true.

DAVID: If you're resting peacefully by the end of this flight, I'll start seeing Madam Kiki myself.

HARVEY: Unfortunately she doesn't give finders fees, but here's her card.

(Takes a card out of his wallet. As he hands the card to DAVID some rose petals fall out of his wallet.)

DAVID: What are those, Zuzu's petals?

HARVEY: These are from a rose that I received for passing my drivers test for the first time.

DAVID: When was this?

HARVEY: Last week. I need a cigarette so badly.

DAVID: Can't Madam Kiki talk you out of smoking?

HARVEY: She wants to, but I'm not ready for that yet.

(Takes a pack of cigarettes out of his pocket as he holds the phone on to his shoulder.)

DAVID: Don't do it.

HARVEY: What are they going to do, kick me out?

DAVID: They hate your guts already. I wouldn't push it.

HARVEY: I'm the customer, and the customer's always right. And right now I need a cigarette.

(FLIGHT ATTENDANT #2 enters.)

FLIGHT ATTENDANT #2: *(To DAVID)* Would you like another drink, Sir?

(HARVEY fumbles to hide his cigarette.)

DAVID: You bet.

(FLIGHT ATTENDANT #2 pours DAVID another drink and hands it to him with some peanuts. DAVID hands her $3.00.)

FLIGHT ATTENDANT #2: Thank you, Sir.

DAVID: Why don't you just leave the cart here?

FLIGHT ATTENDANT #2: Unfortunately I can't do that. *(To HARVEY)* Would you like a drink?

HARVEY: No thank you.

FLIGHT ATTENDANT #2: You're not planning on smoking one of those, I hope.

HARVEY: One of what?

FLIGHT ATTENDANT #2: I didn't think so. *(Starts to walk away. Stops and says to HARVEY)* Enjoy the flight.

HARVEY: I'm going to get her.

DAVID: No, she's going to get you if you smoke one of those cigarettes.

HARVEY: I need a cigarette. I'll blow the smoke down under the seat. She'll never know.

DAVID: Are you kidding? You think nobody's tried that before?

HARVEY: *(Hands DAVID the phone)* Here, hold this. Tell me if you see her coming.

(Bends down as far as he can and lights a cigarette.)

DAVID: God, I feel like I'm back in high school looking out for Nuns.

HARVEY: *(Takes a long hit off his cigarette and sits back in his seat again)* You went to Catholic schools? So did I. Where did you go? I went to Our Lady of Perpetual Help.

DAVID: I went to Our Lady of Beyond Help.

HARVEY: You shouldn't make fun of things like that. They'll hear you.

PILOT: There's something going on out there that shouldn't be, isn't there?

HARVEY: *(Looks up and around)* Oh good Lord, I told you.

DAVID: That's the pilot, you dip shit.

PILOT: You've got two seconds to put out that cigarette.

HARVEY: *(Puts out his cigarette)* How did he know?

PILOT: We have ways.

(Laughs wickedly.)

(FLIGHT ATTENDANT #2 enters. She walks over to HARVEY and holds out her hand. HARVEY puts the pack of cigarettes in her hand. She exits.)

DAVID: Busted!

HARVEY: They're worse than the Nuns. They're worse than my mother.

DAVID: *(Into the phone)* What? Hey, hold on a minute. *(Pause)* No, this sure as Hell ain't Harvey. *(Hands the phone to HARVEY)* It's for you.

HARVEY: Well, what did your tea leaves tell you? *(Pause)* Same as before? Good. Well, now that I've heard it from you again, I'm sure that I will be resting peacefully soon. Thank you so much, Madam Kiki. *(Pause)* What? Hello? *(Looks at the phone, then hangs it up)* I wonder what she meant by that?

DAVID: What?

HARVEY: Right before she hung up, she said, "I will call for you soon."

DAVID: Maybe she's got the hots for you and she's going to call you and ask you to come over and read her tea leaves.

HARVEY: Oh please. No, it wasn't like that. She'll probably call me at home next week to see how the rest of my trip went.

(The bell is heard as the, "Fasten Seat Belt" sign comes on.)

PILOT: Ladies and gentlemen, we are starting our descent into Los Angeles International Airport. Please fasten your seat belt and be sure that your seat backs and tray tables are in the upright position. On behalf of the flight crew and Coastal Airlines, I would like to thank you for choosing to fly with us today, and we hope to see you again soon on Coastal Airlines.

HARVEY: Don't hold your breath. I wouldn't put my life in your hands again if you were the last pilot on earth.

PILOT: That's it. He's mine!

*(A struggle is heard from the cockpit as FLIGHT
ATTENDANTS 1 and 2 hold the pilot back pleading with
him not to leave the cockpit.)*

FLIGHT ATTENDANTS #1 and #2: He's not worth it.
You'll lose your license! You have to land the plane!

HARVEY: He'd better stay right where he is.

DAVID: You call that resting peacefully?

HARVEY: I sure will tonight. Thanks to Madam Kiki, I
feel great!

DAVID: I hope you still feel great when you get your
phone bill.

HARVEY: Whatever it cost, it was worth it.

DAVID: These calls are going to cost you a fortune, you
know.

HARVEY: Now who's being melodramatic? What is it?
Maybe $20.00 for Dr. Panelli and about $15.00 for Madam
Kiki. Big deal.

DAVID: You didn't read the fine print, did you?

HARVEY: What fine print? *(DAVID points to the writing
by the phone)* *(Gasps)* $7.00 a minute! Oh good Lord!
(Pushes the call button repeatedly) *(FLIGHT ATTENDANTS
#1 and #2 enter)* There must be some mistake! *(Points to the
writing by the phone)* This has to be a type-o! This can't be
right!

FLIGHT ATTENDANT #2: $7.00 a minute. That's what
it costs.

HARVEY: Oh, good Lord! I was on for ...

DAVID: Fifteen minutes with the shrink, and about 20
minutes with the phychic.

HARVEY: That's 35 minutes. That's *(Gets out his calculator)* 35 times 7. Holy Mother of God! That's $245.00!

DAVID: *(Laughs)* That's more than the flight cost.

HARVEY: Oh my God! Oh my God! I'm having a heart attack! Help me! Help me!

(His head falls, and he is still.)

DAVID: Harvey? Hey, Harvey.

(Looks at FLIGHT ATTENDANT #1.)

FLIGHT ATTENDANT #1: *(Takes HARVEY's pulse)* He's dead.

DAVID: He kept saying he was going to have a heart attack.

FLIGHT ATTENDANT #1: Poor bastard.

FLIGHT ATTENDANT #2: *(Positions HARVEY to be sitting up with his head back. Puts DAVID's elbow on HARVEY's arm to hold HARVEY in place)* Could you hold him like this so that people getting off the plane will just think he's sleeping?

(Exits)

DAVID: Hold him? The man is dead! I'm not holding a dead man.

FLIGHT ATTENDANT #1: Please. We don't want to upset the other passengers. And he just looks like he's resting. *(Starts to exit. Stops and looks at HARVEY)* He looks so peaceful.

(DAVID looks at HARVEY, then he takes Madam Kiki's card out of his pocket and looks at it. The sound of the plane landing is heard. DAVID fumbles with HARVEY trying to prop him up and tries to put a magazine in HARVEY's hands. He finally gives up and puts HARVEY's coat over HARVEY from the neck down and puts his head up against a pillow.)

PILOT: Ladies and gentlemen, please remain seated until the aircraft has come to a complete stop. For those of you continuing on to Houston, our stop over will be for one hour and 30 minutes. Please exit the airplane and plan to reboard in one hour. I would like to once again thank those of you whose final destination is here in Los Angeles.

END OF PLAY

Set Props:
    One Safety Instruction Card
    Two Barf Bags
    Phone
    Drink Cart with Drinks, Plastic Glasses & Bags of Peanuts
    One Pillow

Hand Props:
    One Safety Instruction Card
    Hand Towel
    One Oxygen Mask
    Microphone
    Seat Belt for Demonstration
    Phone Credit Card
    Barf Bag
    Six One Dollar Bills
    Paper
    Pen
    Calculator
    Brief Case
    One Coin
    Business Card
    Rose Petals
    Pack of Cigarettes

Costumes:
    HARVEY: Overcoat with a Crucifix, a Star of David, a
Scapular, a Buddha Charm (Ho Tai), a Rosary, a Silver
Talisman, a St. Christopher's Medal, Two Bracelets, a Four-
Leaf Clover and a Garlic Necklace
    DAVID: Slacks, Shirt and Sweater
    FLIGHT ATTENDANTS: Blue and White Uniforms

IDENTITY CRISIS

CHARACTERS

ANDREA ESTRIDGE:
Mid 40's, Demanding

NATHAN ROSS:
Around 30 Years Old, Bored with His Job, Impatient

KATHY HEALY:
Late 20's, Cute, Lively

JACK:
Around 40 Years Old

GEORGE:
Around 60 Years Old

MARIAN:
Around 60 Years Old

TIME

Approximately 30 minutes

PLACE

Baggage Claim Area of Nebulas Airlines
at the Oakland Airport

Scene One

ANDREA: *(Pounding on the door of the Lost and Found)* Hello! Hello! *(Opens the door and sees NATHAN sitting at a desk reading a newspaper)* I've been knocking on this door for five minutes!

NATHAN: Why?

ANDREA: This is the lost and found, isn't it?

NATHAN: *(Gets up and looks at the sign on the door)* Yep.

ANDREA: Well, my bag is lost and I want it found!

NATHAN: What flight did you come in on?

ANDREA: Nebulas Airlines, flight 835.

NATHAN: *(Checks a sheet of paper on the desk)* That landed at 12:00.

ANDREA: Yes. And it is now 1:10 and my bag is still missing. Go check the airplane. It has to be there.

NATHAN: All the bags are off the plane.

ANDREA: That's impossible. They obviously missed one. Go look.

NATHAN: All the bags are off the plane. Yours must have been misplaced by the crew when you boarded in Los Angeles.

ANDREA: Look, I don't care where it was misplaced. I want my bag and I want it now!

NATHAN: *(Hands ANDREA a piece of paper)* Fill out this form and we'll try to locate your bag and get it to you as soon as possible.

ANDREA: Are you out of your mind?

67

NATHAN: No.

ANDREA: I'm not filling out any stupid form. I want my bag right now.

NATHAN: I would like nothing better than to give you your bag right now so we can both get on with our lives. Unfortunately, I don't have your bag.

ANDREA: *(Takes a piece of paper and a pen out of her purse. Reads his name on his I.D. badge and writes it down)* Nathan Ross, huh? Well, Nathan Ross, this is not your day. You have crossed the wrong person. I want my bag.

NATHAN: I can't give you what I don't have.

ANDREA: Don't get sarcastic with me you little snot! Do you have any idea who I am?

NATHAN: Not a clue.

ANDREA: I am Andrea Estridge.

NATHAN: I've heard that name. Where have I heard that name?

ANDREA: *Inquiring Minds* newspaper.

NATHAN: You're the Pooper Snooper!

ANDREA: That's right, and if you don't find my bag for me right now, I'm going to write an article about you and your incompetent airline that will blast this company to smithereens!

NATHAN: I'm so scared.

ANDREA: Well, you should be. The pen is mightier than the sword, you know. I could put an end to this conglomerate of blithering idiots with one article.

NATHAN: Right. Why don't you put the article right next to the one you wrote last week about the hound dog that was born with Elvis' head. Everyone believed that one too.

ANDREA: I saw that dog with my own eyes! *(NATHAN laughs)* Everything I write is the truth!

NATHAN: Yeah, and there's no sugar in Pixie Sticks.

ANDREA: If you don't believe it, why do you buy it?

NATHAN: Buy it? I wouldn't waste my money on that trash. My brain-dead roommate buys it. And when she's done with it, I line my bird cage with it. My parrot used to have a problem with constipation, but ever since I've been lining his cage with your crap, he give out more crap than you do.

ANDREA: I want to talk to your supervisor.

NATHAN: Look lady, don't give me a hard time. I've got two guys out on stress leave calling it an ID, so I'm here by myself for the fourth day in a row.

ANDREA: What's an ID?

NATHAN: Injury on duty. They're stressed out and they're calling it an injury on duty.

ANDREA: That's no reason for you to be an asshole to me. I thought that Nebulas Airlines was known as the Friendship Airline.

NATHAN: Yeah, so what?

ANDREA: So you're supposed to be friendly and cooperative like your commercial says.

NATHAN: Yeah, I'm a regular Mr. Rogers.

ANDREA: Then help me get my bag back.

NATHAN: All right, all right. I'll call LAX and see if your bag got left behind. What does it look like?

ANDREA: It's a brown medium-sized suitcase with the initials "A.E." on the top by the clasp.

NATHAN: *(More to himself than to ANDREA)* Sounds like our mystery bag.

ANDREA: What mystery bag?

NATHAN: This one here.

(Goes to the back of the room and brings out a brown suitcase that looks very old and dirty.)

ANDREA: That is certainly not my bag.

NATHAN: I didn't think so. This bag has been here for ten days.

ANDREA: It looks like it's been here for ten years. Why did you call it your mystery bag?

NATHAN: It's not your bag, so don't worry about it, OK?

ANDREA: Come on. What's the story behind this bag?

NATHAN: There is no story. It's just been here a while.

ANDREA: I've been a reporter for over 20 years, Nathan. I know a story when I see it, and this bag has a story. What is it?

NATHAN: No way. If I tell you, you'll go off on this like there's no tomorrow and we'll be reading about it in that goofy newspaper of yours next week.

ANDREA: Sounds good. Keep going.

(Takes a close look at the bag.)

NATHAN: I know nothing.

ANDREA: Hey look! It's got my initials on it.

NATHAN: I had a feeling you'd notice that.

ANDREA: Nobody's called about it or come in to claim it, huh?

NATHAN: No. I'm going to call LAX and ask about your bag.

(Goes to the phone and dials.)

ANDREA: Don't change the subject.

NATHAN: I didn't change the subject. You want your bag, don't you?

ANDREA: *(Still looking at the bag)* Has anybody opened it?

NATHAN: Of course not! *(Speaking into the phone)* Yeah. This is Nathan Ross at Oakland. A bag from flight 835 is missing. You wouldn't happen to have any stragglers that didn't make it on the plane would you? *(Pause)* OK. Just thought I'd check. *(Pause)* Could you fax me a list of all the other flights leaving at the same time as 835 and their destinations? *(Pause)* Thanks. *(Pause)* Yeah. Have a good one.

(Hangs up.)

ANDREA: The clasp looks like it's rusted over. You couldn't open this if you tried.

NATHAN: I know.

ANDREA: I knew you tried, you scum bag. I bet you open every suitcase that gets brought in here.

NATHAN: I do not! Besides, everyone who's seen this bag has tried to open it.

ANDREA: What do you mean everyone who's seen it?

NATHAN: Look, why don't we just worry about your bag and forget about this one.

(As he is picking up the bag, the door opens and KATHY enters and hands NATHAN a fax.)

KATHY: This just came in for you.

NATHAN: Thanks. Could you call these guys on this list and ask them if any of them have found a brown medium-sized suitcase with the initials AE on it that belonged on flight 835?

KATHY: Where's the form?

NATHAN: There is no form.

KATHY: You didn't have them fill out a form?

ANDREA: I am not filling out any of your forms. I want my bag.

KATHY: So it's your bag that's lost?

ANDREA: That's right. And I'm not leaving here until it is found.

KATHY: Hey, did somebody finally claim that bag? *(Looks at ANDREA and points to the old suitcase)* Is it yours?

NATHAN: No, it's not hers.

ANDREA: No, but if you don't find mine, maybe I'll take this one instead.

KATHY: You don't look like Amelia Earhart to me.

ANDREA: Amelia Earhart?

KATHY: Yeah. *(To NATHAN)* Did you tell her?

NATHAN: No, Big Mouth, I didn't tell her.

ANDREA: What's this about Amelia Earhart?

NATHAN: Nothing.

KATHY: Oh, come on. It's no secret. Everybody knows.

NATHAN: If you tell *her,* everybody will know.

ANDREA: Tell me what?

NATHAN: Let's try to find your bag.

ANDREA: You try to find my bag. Put that down. *(NATHAN puts the bag down and goes back to his desk. ANDREA reads KATHY's name tag as she picks up the bag, and leads KATHY away from NATHAN)* Come here, Kathy Healy.

NATHAN: Be careful what you say to her. She's the Pooper Snooper from *Inquiring Minds.*

KATHY: You're kidding! I don't believe it! This is so cool!

NATHAN: Yeah, real cool. Whatever you say to her is going to be twisted and magnified 50 times, so watch it.

ANDREA: Don't pay any attention to him, Kathy. Why don't you and I have a nice little chat about this suitcase.

KATHY: What do you want to know?

ANDREA: Whatever you know. Where did the bag come from?

KATHY: That I don't know, but then we never do.

ANDREA: What do you mean you never do?

KATHY: Every time it comes in, it comes from a different place.

ANDREA: Every time?

KATHY: Yeah. This is about the sixth or seventh time this bag has been in Oakland.

ANDREA: And it always comes to Nebulas Airlines?

KATHY: No. It never comes in on the same airline or from the same city.

ANDREA: Then you know where it comes from.

KATHY: Not exactly. It snows up on a conveyor belt with the other bags from a flight and ends up in the Lost and Found because nobody claims it When whoever gets it in the Lost and Found calls the baggage claim area in the airport the flight originated from, they say that the bag didn't come from there. And it never has a baggage claim ticket on it either.

ANDREA: This has happened six or seven times before with this same bag?

KATHY: Yeah. And that's just in Oakland. Weird, huh?

ANDREA: Wait. I don't get it. Who comes to claim it?

KATHY: Nobody.

ANDREA: If nobody claims it, it would never leave the Lost and Found, so how can it keep coming back?

KATHY: That's part of the mystery. We don't know

where it goes. All of a sudden it's just gone. Then, just as suddenly, a couple of months later, it's back.

ANDREA: How bizarre.

KATHY: No kidding.

ANDREA: What was that you said about Amelia Earhart earlier?

KATHY: The initials A.E. are on the bag, and with such a weird story about it appearing and disappearing, someone started saying that maybe it belonged to Amelia Earhart. Add a little spookiness to the story, I guess.

ANDREA: It works.

KATHY: Yeah. Especially when you look at the bag. It looks so old and like it's been through Hell and back again – and again, and again.

ANDREA: And the bag just shows up in different airports?

KATHY: Yeah. It's been all over the place.

ANDREA: It's almost like it's searching for something – or *someone.*

(Pause – then KATHY and ANDREA say simultaneously)

KATHY & ANDREA: It's owner!

ANDREA: I love it! This is great! Let me get this down.

(Takes the paper and pen out and starts writing as she paces back and forth.)

KATHY: Make sure you spell my name right in the paper.

NATHAN: So you gave her the story?

KATHY: Yeah. I've been dying to tell someone.

NATHAN: I knew you couldn't keep your mouth shut about this. Oh well, it was bound to come out sooner or later. It might as well be from you. You sure picked the right person to tell. This will be plastered all over the front page of her tacky tabloid next week.

KATHY: Hey, look at it this way. I got her off your back, didn't I?

ANDREA: No, Ms. Healy. you did not get me off his back. I want my bag – especially now.

NATHAN: Why especially now?

ANDREA: I need what's in there right away.

KATHY: Is there some kind of medication in your bag?

ANDREA: Something like that. All this talk about ghostly suitcases, and now with mine missing, I'm getting very nervous. And believe me, you don't want me to have an anxiety attack.

NATHAN: You mean you didn't?

ANDREA: If I did, you wouldn't have to ask.

NATHAN: I bet that's right.

ANDREA: Find it, please! I need my lotion and my balls. *(NATHAN looks at her inquisitively)* I have iron balls.

NATHAN: *(Under his breath)* More like brass.

ANDREA: Chinese Iron Balls, you nimrod! They help me relax. All of my tranquillity products are in that bag too. I need my aromatherapy.

NATHAN: Aromatherapy?

ANDREA: Yes. Products that use your sense of smell to enhance and stimulate your mind and body. Don't tell me you've never heard of this concept.

NATHAN: Yeah, I've heard of it. On TV they call it smell-o-vision. It's great on cable, especially certain channels.

KATHY: Nathan! Aromaology is a very advanced study. There are lots of books about it. You should read one.

NATHAN: Books? I can see it now. Feeling anxious or neurotic? Turn to page 45 and scratch and sniff your troubles away. I saw that in *Hustler* once.

ANDREA: You ignoramus!

NATHAN: *(Laughs)* Aromatherapy.

KATHY: Cool it, Nathan. I use aromatherapy products too.

NATHAN: You would.

KATHY: It's very good for you. Aromaology is the art and science of pure flower and plant essences. Stress and lots of the most common illnesses are a direct result of the pressures we face every day that effect our nervous system. Aromatherapy is a pure and natural way of healing ourselves.

NATHAN: That's what doctors are for.

ANDREA: Doctors don't know diddly squat!

NATHAN: Hey, don't knock doctors. Some of my best friends are doctors. *(The phone rings and NATHAN answers it)* Yeah? *(Pause)* Oh my God! What are you guys smoking out there? *(Pause)* Why didn't you call me the minute this happened? *(Pause)* Get those bags out on the next plane! *(Slams the phone down and says to KATHY)* Are you ready for this? Miami's really outdone themselves this time. Whoever handled the bags for flight 5716 put them on the inbound belt instead of the outbound.

KATHY: So the bags are still in Miami?

NATHAN: Yeah. Man, when 5716 lands, we're going to have 300 really pissed off people on our hands. Wait till they find out that their bags won't be here for another six hours.

KATHY: What time is 5716 coming in?

NATHAN: It just landed.

KATHY: What? Oh my God!

NATHAN: Man, their Team Leader's in a butt load of trouble.

KATHY: *(Says as if she knows that NATHAN has done this in the past)* I can't imagine causing such a screw up. Can you?

NATHAN: Hey, it was only my second day on the job. Give me a break.

KATHY: *(Laughs)* I'm going to start calling these guys to see if they have your bag.

(Starts making phone calls, one after another, talking quietly.)

ANDREA: Good. Is there another phone I can use?

NATHAN: Is it a local call? *(ANDREA holds up her telephone credit card) (NATHAN points to the other desk)* Over there.

ANDREA: *(Goes to the other phone and dials)* Ted? It's me. *(Pause)* No. I'm at the airport. *(Pause)* Oakland. *(Pause)* One of my bags is missing, but never mind that now.

NATHAN: *(Overhears ANDREA and jokingly says to KATHY)* Never mind? Great! We can quit looking for her bag. I'm going to lunch.

ANDREA: I wasn't talking to you. You keep looking. *(Walks around to desk so her back is to NATHAN and KATHY and says into the phone)* I've stumbled on the best story I've had in a long time. *(Pause)* I'll fill you in later. Right now I need you to do something for me. Go to my May, 1993 files. I think it was the second or third week of May. Look up the piece about the pilot who said that Amelia Earhart talked him down on Howland Island when he lost contact with the control tower on his way to Hawaii. *(Pause)* I want you to fax it to my hotel. *(Pause)* Yeah, I have a great follow-up to that. *(Pause)* Thanks, kiddo. See you next week. *(Hangs up and says to

NATHAN) You know, I just remembered something. I lost a bag last year that was never found. I wonder if this is it.

NATHAN: I'm sure it isn't.

ANDREA: How do you know? It's so beat up, it's hard to tell, and even you said it sounded like mine.

NATHAN: You just remembered you lost a bag last year?

ANDREA: Yeah. I forgot all about it. All it had in it was some underwear and a couple of sweaters, so it wasn't that big of a deal when it got lost.

NATHAN: Nice try, lady, but you're not getting that bag.

ANDREA: Hey, that might be my bag. You can't keep it here if I'm claiming it.

NATHAN: Saying it *might* be your bag is not claiming it, and I can't let just anybody open lost luggage.

ANDREA: If you could get it open, we could see whether that's my underwear in there.

NATHAN: Now there's an attractive thought.

ANDREA: I wouldn't let a pervert like you look at my underwear. I'll look inside and tell you whether it's mine or not.

NATHAN: Oh, and I just take your word for it, right?

ANDREA: Right.

NATHAN: Wrong.

ANDREA: I bet airport security would make you open it for me.

NATHAN: *(Laughs)* Airport security?

ANDREA: That's right, Mr. Ross. I'm going to go get airport security.

NATHAN: You do that. *(ANDREA exits) (KATHY hangs up from one of her phone calls)* Can you believe her?

KATHY: Where'd she go?

NATHAN: She tried to tell me that this is her bag that she lost last year.

KATHY: What? She just wants to see what's inside it.

NATHAN: I know.

KATHY: Where is she?

NATHAN: Get this. She went to get airport security to have them make me open it so she can say that it's hers.

KATHY: Oh for God's sake!

NATHAN: Man, if that don't beat all.

KATHY: Security is just going to laugh at her.

NATHAN: No shit. I'm going to put this thing away.

(Brings the suitcase back into the other room and returns.)
(GEORGE and MARIAN enter the Lost and Found.)

GEORGE: I'd like to know when our bags are going to get here.

NATHAN: I take it you were on Nebulas Airlines, flight 5716.

GEORGE: That's right.

JACK: *(Enters and says to GEORGE)* Sir, I told you, your bags would not be at the Lost and Found area. There was an unfortunate mix-up at the Miami airport and your bags are on their way now.

GEORGE: When will they get here?

JACK: As I said before, they'll be arriving at 7:30 this evening.

GEORGE: This is totally unacceptable. I am the Vice President of Security of Courtney Productions. If my bags are lost, you will be hearing from my attorney.

NATHAN: Your attorney? Look, mister, you'll get your bags back tonight.

JACK: Sir, your bags will be arriving safely at 7:30.

GEORGE: They'll probably end up in Honolulu.

NATHAN: *(Under his breath)* That could be arranged.

JACK: Sir, I'm sorry you were inconvenienced, but I'm sure your bags will be here on time tonight.

GEORGE: On time? You call six hours late on time?

MARIAN: George, please. It's not his fault. This man did not misplace our bags.

GEORGE: I don't care. He's here and they're not.

(NATHAN laughs.)

MARIAN: George, remember your blood pressure.

GEORGE: How can I remember my blood pressure? My pills are in my bag and my bag is in Miami!

MARIAN: George, please. Let's just go to the hotel and rest for a couple of hours. Then we'll have a nice dinner and come back and get the bags.

GEORGE: But I can't even take a shower and change my clothes.

MARIAN: I know. It's OK. We can do that later. By 9:00 tonight, we'll be back at the hotel with all our luggage, and everything will be fine.

GEORGE: It better be.

MARIAN: It will be. You'll see.

GEORGE: Marian, from now on we go out of Ft. Lauderdale. We're never flying out of Miami again. Every time we fly out of Miami, something either gets screwed up or disappears.

(GEORGE and MARIAN start to exit.)

NATHAN: Well, that was semi-easy.

MARIAN: *(Turns and says to NATHAN)* No thanks to you, asshole.

(Exits)

NATHAN: God, what is this? That's the second person today who's called me an asshole. *(KATHY and JACK both look at NATHAN and then turn away as if they're trying to avoid saying something)* Oh, shut up!

KATHY: *(Laughs)* I'm going to go finish making these phone calls.

NATHAN: *(To JACK)* Where are the rest of them?

JACK: The rest of who?

NATHAN: From 5716. Am I going to get to talk to all 300 of them?

JACK: No. I got the brunt of it upstairs. Believe me. You were spared.

NATHAN: Why you? You don't work for Nebulus.

JACK: They sent me up to be there when the guy at the gate told them the bad news just in case somebody decided to shoot the messenger.

NATHAN: Anybody try?

JACK: Yeah – all 300. Boy were they mad! Most of them just stormed out screaming that they were never going to fly Nebulas Airlines again.

NATHAN: Won't break my heart.

(AMY enters the Lost and Found. She is actually ANDREA in disguise wearing a short brown wig and brown clothes, using a Southern accent and a pleasant voice.)

AMY: Excuse me. I hate to bother you, but my suitcase

was lost about a week and a half ago, and I think it might be here.

NATHAN: Where's your baggage claim ticket?

AMY: I don't have one. I lost the bag before I boarded the flight.

NATHAN: Why did you wait so long to come and claim it?

AMY: I just returned from the trip I was taking the day I lost my bag.

NATHAN: What does it look like?

AMY: It's brown, medium size, and has my initials on the top.

NATHAN: What are your initials?

AMY: A.E.

(NATHAN knocks KATHY on the arm and points to AMY. KATHY hangs up the phone.)

NATHAN: Your initials are A.E.?

AMY: Yes, sir. My name is Amy Eberhart.

(NATHAN goes into the other room and brings out the suitcase.)

NATHAN: Is this your bag?

AMY: That's it!

NATHAN: I think we have a winner!

(Starts to hand the suitcase to AMY.)

KATHY: Nathan! Wait a minute. I'm sorry, ma'am, but could I see some I.D.?

AMY: What for? All I want is my bag.

KATHY: I know. We'll get this settled as quickly as possible. But we can't release a bag without at least one form of I.D. and proof of ownership.

AMY: Well, why don't you open it up and I'll tell you what's in it.

KATHY: We can't. The clasp is rusted and it won't open.

NATHAN: *(Quickly hits KATHY on the arm and cuts in)* At least it looks like it won't open, but let's give it a try.

(Tries to open the bag, but can't)

KATHY: I'm sorry, ma'am, but we can't release the bag without proper proof of ownership.

NATHAN: Excuse us a minute. *(Leads KATHY away from AMY and whispers)* Look, here's our chance to get rid of this bag once and for all. Then when that bitch comes back, we can tell her to go screw herself.

KATHY: Your people skills are astounding.

NATHAN: I do my best.

KATHY: OK, but at least let's fill out the form and get her name and address just in case there are any problems.

NATHAN: With who? Ms. Pooper Snooper?

KATHY: She's not exactly your number one fan, you know. And she could cause a lot of problems for us if she wanted to.

NATHAN: Let her. Everything she prints is lies and trash anyway. Nobody with half a brain believes anything she writes, let alone reads it. *(Laughs)* Let's tell her Amelia Earhart came and picked up the bag.

KATHY: Right. We should have that lady fill this out though. *(Takes a form out of the desk drawer and says to*

AMY) Ma'am, we need to fill out this form before we can release the bag.

AMY: *(Looks upset and then composes herself)* You know, I'd love to oblige you, but I'm really in a hurry. Can I come back and do that later?

NATHAN: Sure. We'll be here. *(NATHAN and AMY both reach for the bag)* You can have the bag when we get the form filled out.

AMY: I really don't have time for this. Please give me my bag.

KATHY: I'm sorry, but we can't do that. I'm sure you understand the security problems we could run into if we did.

AMY: *(Losing the southern accent)* Do you understand the legal problems you could run in to if you don't? *(Calms down and uses the accent again)* I'm sorry. This has been a very tough day for me, and like I said, I'm in a hurry.

(KATHY and NATHAN look at each other suspiciously.)

NATHAN: Can I see your I.D.?
AMY: I have to go.

(Starts to leave.)

NATHAN: *(Pulls her wig off)* Nice try, lady.
KATHY: Oh my God!
NATHAN: *(To ANDREA)* What is your problem?
ANDREA: *(Using her regular voice again)* Nothing! What is your problem?
NATHAN: You! What do you want with this bag?
ANDREA: I've come to claim it.
NATHAN: Claim this!

KATHY: Nathan, calm down. Ma'am, please stay right here. *(Calls outside)* Jack?

(JACK enters.)

ANDREA: What is it with you people? Just give me the goddamn bag!

JACK: Alright, everybody just calm down. Now, what's going on here?

ANDREA: They have my bag and they won't give it to me.

NATHAN: This is not her bag. She just wants to see what's in it.

JACK: Why?

NATHAN: So she can write a stupid article for her stupid tabloid.

JACK: Huh?

KATHY: She's the Pooper Snooper.

JACK: The what?

KATHY: The Pooper Snooper.

JACK: What the Hell is that?

KATHY: She's a reporter for *Inquiring Minds* newspaper.

NATHAN: A reporter? Clark Kent just rolled over in his grave.

ANDREA: You make one more crack about my profession and I'm going to sue you.

NATHAN: You call making up stupid stories that nobody believes a profession?

ANDREA: And I suppose you call yourself a professional. Look at the way you talk to your customers. Whatever happened to, "The customer's always right."?

NATHAN: When they're right, I say they're right.

ANDREA: I'm right.

NATHAN: You're nuts.

ANDREA: You're an asshole.

NATHAN: It's a blessing.

ANDREA: Yeah well, like they say, the smaller the dick, the bigger the asshole.

NATHAN: *(To JACK)* Make her go away.

ANDREA: Just give me the bag and I'll leave you alone.

NATHAN: There's no way you're getting this bag.

JACK: Ma'am, we can't release a bag without proof of ownership. That's airport policy.

ANDREA: How can I prove it's my bag without a baggage claim ticket or looking inside?

NATHAN: Well now, that is a problem, isn't it?

JACK: And I thought 5716 was going to be the headache of the day.

ANDREA: What did you say about 5716?

JACK: That's a flight from Miami that's also having luggage problems.

ANDREA: Flight 5716 from Miami? This is too much of a coincidence. 5716 is Amelia Earhart's Pilot License number, and her last flight originated in Miami.

NATHAN: What is this obsession you have with Amelia Earhart?

ANDREA: I'm fascinated by her. She was light years ahead of her time.

NATHAN: She's been dead for 60 years. Let her rest in peace.

ANDREA: You don't know that.

NATHAN: I hate to break it to you, but they called off the search.

ANDREA: They never proved that she died.

NATHAN: Lady, her plane went down in the middle of the Pacific Ocean in 1937. I think it's safe to say she's dead.

ANDREA: I think finding her suitcase would give us the evidence we need to know for sure.

KATHY: Where do you expect to find her suitcase?

ANDREA: I don't know. That's why I look everywhere. I have to know what happened.

NATHAN: You assume to be a writer. Make up your own ending. *(Pause)* Wait a minute. The light bulb just went on. That's what you're doing, isn't it? You want to find her suitcase so bad, I bet you planted this one just to say it's hers so you can have that story. "I Have Amelia Earhart's Suitcase." Page one. Centerfold. You wanted to get a whole bunch of people to see this bag and notice it appearing and disappearing and get them talking about how mysterious it is. You probably even started the rumor that it belonged to Amelia Earhart to plant the seed for your story.

KATHY: That's why you're trying to claim the bag. You know it's a fake, and you want to get rid of it while there's still a mystery attached to it, so it fits your story.

NATHAN: Yeah, it's easy to plant a suitcase in a baggage claim area, especially with a carousel full of other bags.

KATHY: I'm going to go into the other room and finish making those phone calls.

(Exits with the bag.)

JACK: Why would you go to all this trouble?

ANDREA: For the story of the century.

JACK: But it's her flight bag that's missing, not a suitcase.

ANDREA: What? Amelia Earhart always wore the same clothes? No change of underwear?

NATHAN: You want to find Amelia Earhart's underwear, and you call *me* a pervert?

ANDREA: I want that bag. I need a story that will boost my credibility. People are a lot smarter than they used to be. They're tired of reading about dogs with Elvis' head and Prince Charles' sons being born with the ears of a rabbit and secret operations to make them look normal. They want something more tangible, something they can identify with and believe.

NATHAN: Then write for a real newspaper. Screw tabloids.

ANDREA: People also want sensationalism and excitement. Fiction is a lot more fun and exciting than fact.

KATHY: *(Enters)* I've called everybody on the list and nobody has your bag.

ANDREA: *(Hugs KATHY)* It's people like you who make tabloids so much fun to write for.

KATHY: Wait a minute. You didn't lose a bag today.

ANDREA: I'm sorry you wasted all that time. But that shows you how well a good story can work.

KATHY: Now that we know it's a fake, just out of curiosity, what's in the suitcase?

ANDREA: Just some old clothes.

KATHY: Do you have the key?

ANDREA: No, but I bet this will work.

(Takes out a Swiss Army knife.)

KATHY: I'll go get the suitcase. Let's see if this works.

ANDREA: It'll be like opening a time capsule. *(KATHY returns with the suitcase and ANDREA opens it with the knife)*

Hey, it worked! Let's see what I put in here. *(She starts looking through the clothes while everyone else looks on. She comes across a map and opens it up)* I don't remember putting a map in here. What is this? *(She studies the map for a minute)* Oh my God! This map is marked with the route Amelia Earhart was following on her last flight. Where did this come from?

KATHY: *(Laughs)* Come on. You put that in there just in case somebody opened it so it would go along with your story.

ANDREA: No I didn't. I swear to God. I have never seen this map before in my life. Look how old it looks. Oh my God! Do you realize ... I got to go. It's been fun. Bye.

(Starts to leave with the map.)

NATHAN: Where do you think you're going? Give me the map.

ANDREA: No way. This was in my suitcase, so it's my map.

NATHAN: We don't know that that's your suitcase.

ANDREA: I just told you it was.

NATHAN: You also told us you saw a dog with Elvis' head.

(Grabs the map from ANDREA.)

ANDREA: Give me that map!

(Goes after NATHAN and they start fighting for the map.)

JACK: OK, break it up you two. *(Separates ANDREA and NATHAN and takes the map)* Nobody's taking this map anywhere. *(JACK gives the map to KATHY. KATHY throws the map to NATHAN and he throws it back to her while ANDREA tries to get it. ["Keep Away" style])* I think you've caused enough trouble for one day. Let's go.

ANDREA: I'm not going anywhere till I get that map.

JACK: *(Takes ANDREA by the arm, starts to lead her to the door)* You're going to go to jail if you don't leave right now.

ANDREA: *(Starts fighting back)* Give me my bag!

NATHAN: You've lied about that bag right from the start. I bet it's not even yours.

ANDREA: I can't prove it, but it's mine. *(JACK drags ANDREA to the door)* What do you want from me?

NATHAN: I want the truth.

ANDREA: *(As JACK drags her out the door)* You can't handle the truth!

NATHAN: This is the screwiest day I've had in a long time! *(Looks at the map)* Where did this come from anyway?

KATHY: You're not the only one around here with a sense of humor, you know.

NATHAN: You put that in there? *(KATHY smiles)* How'd you get it open?

KATHY: I have a Swiss Army knife too.

NATHAN: I knew that there was more to you than meets the eye.

KATHY: And what's wrong with what meets the eye?

NATHAN: Not a damn thing.

(KATHY and NATHAN hug.)

THE END

Set Props:
Paper with List of Flights
Lost and Found Form
Old, Dirty, Medium Size Brown Suitcase with Initials
    "A.E." on it
Two Sweaters and a Map in Suitcase
Two Desks
Two Phones

Hand Props:
Fax with List of Flights
Swiss Army Knife

Costumes:
NATHAN: Gray Uniform with Name Tag
KATHY: Blue Uniform with Name Tag
ANDREA: Red Dress with Matching Hat, Ornate Jewelry
AMY: Brown Wig, Brown Shirt and Pants
JACK: Security Guard's Uniform with Name Tag
GEORGE: Brown Suit and Tie
MARIAN: White Dress and Sweater

www.ingramcontent.com/pod-product-compliance
Lightning Source LLC
Chambersburg PA
CBHW071929130726
47909CB00014B/2785

Whistling Pirates

Whistling Pines book 5

Dean L. Hovey

Print ISBNs
Amazon Print 978 0 2286 1732 7
LSI Print 9780228617334
B&N Print 978022867341
Ingram Spark 9780228627708

BWL Publishing Inc.

Books we love to write ...
Authors around the world.

http://bwlpublishing.ca